To order additional copies of this book, contact:
Xlibris
844-714-8691
www.Xlibris.com
Orders@Xlibris.com

ISBN: Softcover   978-1-6641-4228-2
       Hardcover   978-1-6641-4229-9
       EBook   978-1-6641-4227-5

Library of Congress Control Number: 2020922486

Print information available on the last page

Rev. date: 11/16/2020

My Antelope Loves Cantaloupe

Robert Kegan

Illustrated by:
Joan Walsh

For Jack And Sam, Who Love

-Wait For It

Rack Of Lamb!

My Antelope...

...Loves Cantaloupe!

My Pekingese...

...Loves Mac And Cheese!

My Palominos...

...Love Jalapenos!

My Labrador...

...Loves Albacore!

My Honking Goose...

...Loves Chocolate Mousse!

My Beagle And fox...

...Love Bagel and Lox!

My Wild Stallions...

...Love Mild Scallions!

My Wide-eyed
Poodles...

...Love Stir-fried
Noodles!

My Leopard Cubs...

...Love Peppered Subs!

My Red-Billed Parrots...

...Love Char-Grilled Carrots!

My Duck And Bunny...

...Love Buckwheat
Honey!

My Hand-Raised Lamb...

...Loves Pan-Glazed
Ham!

My Gorilla...

...Loves Sarsaparilla!

My Spotted Pigs...

...Love Potted Figs!

My Armadillos..

...Love
Marshmallows!

My Schnoodle...

...Loves Strudel!

And Finally, Say This Plover And Hen...

"Now read this book
all over again!

Have someone read you
The first half of each pair.
Now, do you remember
The rhyme that is there?"

CPSIA information can be obtained
at www.ICGtesting.com
Printed in the USA
BVHW022325050121
597069BV00002B/16